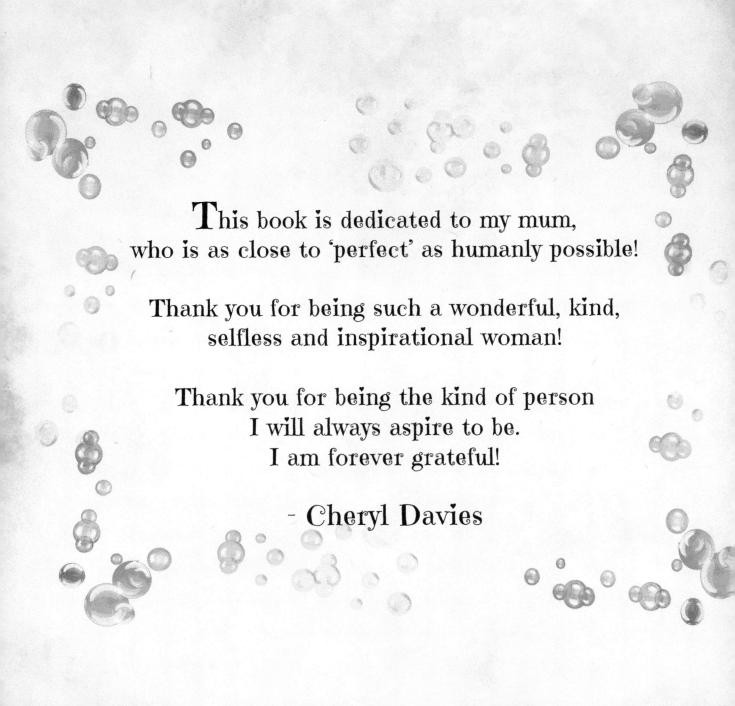

This book is dedicated to my mum,
who is as close to 'perfect' as humanly possible!

Thank you for being such a wonderful, kind,
selfless and inspirational woman!

Thank you for being the kind of person
I will always aspire to be.
I am forever grateful!

- Cheryl Davies

# This book is given with love:

_____

_____

# The Perfect Potion

By
Cheryl Davies

Illustrated by
Jenny Yevheniia Lisovaya

The cauldron bubbled rapidly,
little Charm sat near and purred,
Luna watched her sister, Astrid Gale,
as the cauldron was now stirred.

Rainbow bubbles popped intensely,
as they jumped from out the pot.
Astrid made sure no ingredient,
was neither missing nor forgot.

Every item was measured
and checked again as it went in.
Perfectly the spell was spoken,
so the magic could begin!

Little Luna watched intently,
as rainbow steam now filled the air.
Her sister made amazing potions.
Oh, how she wished she had Astrid's flair!

"Maybe I can help you, Astrid?"
Luna desperately called out.
Her request was denied flatly.
"No way my little sprout!

You know that you're always a jinx
each time you attempt a spell.
Perhaps you could start reading books?
Maybe then you can excel!"

Luna sadly asked her sister,
"Can't you play with me instead?"
"I'm too busy," Astrid replied,
adding cherries, bright and red!

With an aching, heavy heart
Luna tearfully slouched away.
Luna could not understand,
why Astrid didn't want to play.

Soon a thought appeared to Luna,
whilst up at the stars she gazed.
"I can make a spell for snow,
Astrid will be amazed!

We will play together happily,
hundreds of snowballs we will throw!
Toboggan down the mountainside,
and make witches out of snow."

Luna quickly made her potion.
"I can't wait for all the fun!"
Luna really tried her hardest,
nimbly 'round the room she spun.

She added spices delicately,
with great attention all along,
Luna was determined this time
that her spell would not go wrong.

Luna held her potion tightly,
as she ran to Astrid Gale,
the fabulous and amazing witch,
who was never known to fail!

And when her potion was released,
special magic words were cast.
White snow now covered all the ground,
perfect snowflakes floated past....

Astrid shrieked and leapt out the door.
"What an incredible spell!"
But alas, it wasn't what it seemed,
'cause it was not snow that fell.

Instead of snow within the air,
sticky goo now floated down.
When the witches finally realized,
their happy smiles became a frown.

Stickiness was everywhere,
the glue blanket swept the floor.
They found themselves completely stuck,
to the ground outside their door!

"Really, Luna? Not again!
If only you could get things right..."
"I'm really sorry!" Luna cried,
"I tried with all my might."

Astrid said some magic words,
which took the goo away.
She headed inside and shouted back,
"Don't you bother me! Okay?

I never want to play again,
I don't care if you are sad!"
Luna hoped to please her sister,
but instead, she'd made her mad!

Luna stared out through her window,
and tears trickled down her face,
but she quickly stopped her crying,
after having breathing space.

Luna wasn't giving in.
"It's going to be okay!
I will make my sister laugh,
there's still time to save the day!"

So, Luna puzzled long and hard,
how to make her sister happy.
Tickling might just do the trick,
but she'd need a hand from Flappy.

Flappy was a stunning raven,
feather hues of black and blue.
"Do you have some feathers spare?"
Flappy gladly said, "I do!"

Luna set off to the kitchen,
holding feathers in her hand,
Flappy flew on overhead,
Luna snuck up as she'd planned.

She tickled Astrid everywhere,
and Astrid roared with laughter.
Astrid then shouted, "Luna, STOP!"
But could not prevent disaster.

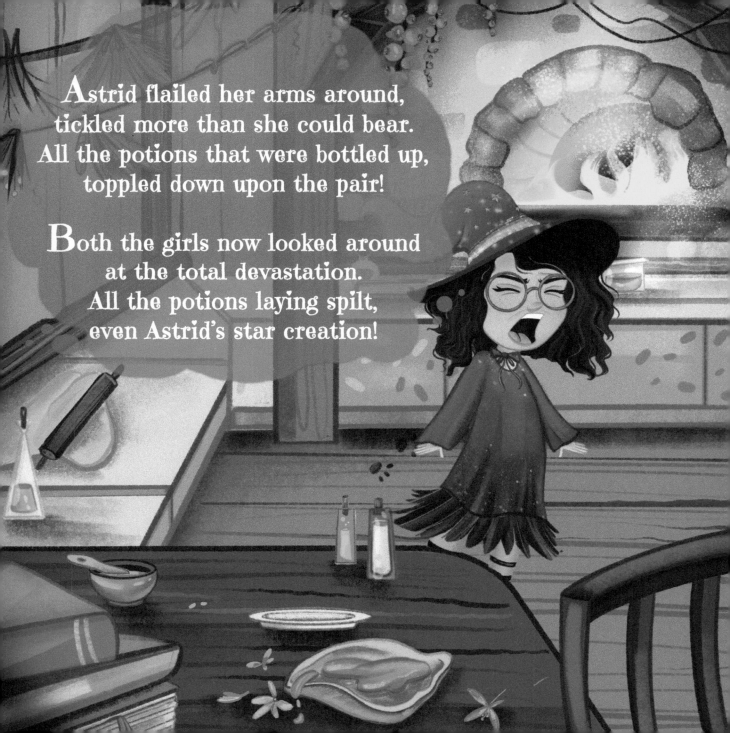

Astrid flailed her arms around,
tickled more than she could bear.
All the potions that were bottled up,
toppled down upon the pair!

Both the girls now looked around
at the total devastation.
All the potions laying spilt,
even Astrid's star creation!

Astrid shrieked, "Just go away!
I need to set this straight,
I never want to play again,
I'm your sister, not your mate!"

Luna ran off into her room.
"How did everything go wrong?"
Flappy flew off after her,
lovingly he tagged along.

Luna cried out, "I am hopeless!
I forever seem to fail...
How I wish I could be perfect,
like my sister Astrid Gale."

Luna had one last idea,
to try a spell for PERFECTION
"This will be the Perfect Potion,
to gain Astrid Gale's attention."

Luna's Perfect Potion sparkled,
under light beams from the moon.
Luna scooped some liquid out,
with a magic, silver spoon.

But before she sipped the potion,
Luna saw her door ajar.
Astrid then came bursting in,
after watching from afar!

"What's this?" Astrid questioned,
spying magic in the pan.
Taken back now by surprise,
Luna halted in her plan.

"I have made a special potion,
so I can be just like you."
Luna quietly admitted this,
pouring back her special brew.

"Oh, Luna," Astrid replied,
"I should not have been so mean!
You're a wonderful young witch,
with a heart that should be seen!

You're doing amazing, Luna,
you're a rising witchling star!
Everyone has to get things wrong,
keep on going and you'll go far!"

Luna listened carefully.
"I can be happy being me?"
Astrid nodded and hugged her sister,
"Are you kidding? Absolutely!

I'm so sorry that I shouted,
and told you to go away.
Please can you forgive me, Luna?
We can still go out to play!

Working hard is important,
but love and friendship's what we need!
Making mistakes is how we grow."
And at last, they both agreed.

Luna took her untouched potion,
and she poured it all away.
"I guess I don't need the Perfect Potion,
now let's go out and play!"

Astrid took her sister's hand,
and they stepped out into the dark.
They leap-frogged and played broomstick tag,
as they whizzed around the park.

Both of them had so much fun,
as the night turned into day.
Hand in hand they flew together,
each perfect in their own way.

# THE END

# Claim your FREE Gift!

 Visit:

# PDICBooks.com/Gift

Thank you for purchasing

# The Perfect Potion

and welcome to the Puppy Dogs & Ice Cream family.
We're certain you're going to love the little gift
we've prepared for you at the website above.

CPSIA information can be obtained
at www.ICGtesting.com
Printed in the USA
LVHW070714201021
700885LV00001B/1

9 781956 462258